I AM READING

Scaredy Dog!

WRITTEN AND ILLUSTRATED BY

ANDY ELLIS

KINGFISHER

BOSTON

For Pedro and all the cats

KINGFISHER
a Houghton Mifflin Company imprint
222 Berkeley Street
Boston, Massachusetts 02116
www.houghtonmifflinbooks.com

First published in 2006
2 4 6 8 10 9 7 5 3 1

Text and illustrations copyright © Andy Ellis 2006

LIBRARY OF CONGRESS CATALOGING-IN-PUBLICATION DATA
has been applied for.

ISBN-13: 978-0-7534-6028-3
ISBN-10: 0-7534-6028-9

Printed in China
1TR/0506/WKT/SCHOY/115MA/C

Contents

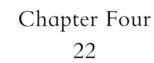
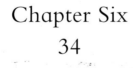

Chapter One

This is Dudley.

Dudley lived with Daphne.

Dudley loved Daphne.

Daphne loved Dudley right back.

Every day Dudley took Daphne
for a run in the park.
They chased planes and dug for
dinosaur bones.

This tired Daphne out!

Chapter Two

Now, for a dog,
Dudley had quite
an imagination.
For instance, he
imagined that
he wasn't scared
of spiders.

But when a spider scuttled across the bedroom floor, it seemed like just the right time to look for lost teddy bears under the covers.

"You're a scaredy dog, Dudley,"
Daphne said with a laugh, and she
gave him a hug. "Don't worry.
I'll save you!"

Dudley dived back under the covers. There, in the dark, Dudley couldn't help imagining all of the other things that scared him silly!

"There are wasps and bees," Dudley
whispered, "and you can't forget
ghosts and vampires. Oh, and big,
blue, hairy boggles, with googly eyes!"

Of course, Dudley had never actually seen a big, blue, hairy boggle, but that wasn't going to stop him from being scared of them.

There was one real scary monster that
Dudley didn't have to imagine.
He was a dog named Attila, and he
was all snarls and pointy teeth.
He lived two doors down,
at Number 48.
There, in the front yard, come rain
or shine, was Attila, tied to a tattered
old piece of rope.

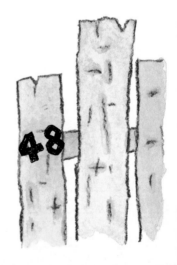

Daphne never mentioned Attila.

And she always walked the long way

to the park so that Dudley didn't have

to go past Number 48.

Chapter Three

One day Dudley and Daphne were watching television when a doggy show came on.

All of the dogs on television were brave and heroic.

Dudley went and looked in the mirror.

Oh, dear. Dudley didn't look brave and heroic.

But then he made a big decision. Dudley decided he wouldn't be scared anymore.

He would try to be brave and heroic, like the dogs on television. He pressed his nose against the misty glass.

"Being brave and heroic can't be that hard," he said to himself.

Suddenly, he heard his favorite word.

"Walkies!" cried Daphne.

In the blink of an eye, they were off

down the road toward the park.

When it came time to cross the street, Daphne and Dudley knew just what to do.

"Stop!" said Daphne. "And look . . . and listen . . . and if there are no cars coming, walk quickly across the street, looking and listening as you go."

Daphne smiled at Dudley, but Dudley
didn't notice.

His head was full of daring doggy deeds.

Chapter Four

They walked through the park gates.

"Come on, Dudley," cried Daphne.

"This looks like a good place to find

some dinosaur bones."

But Dudley had other things on his mind.

"Dudley, the brave and heroic dog, looks around for heroic things to do!" he said to himself.

Suddenly, Dudley saw a sweet little girl all alone on a lonely mountaintop.

"Dudley, the brave rescue dog, will save the day!" he barked.

But it turned out that the sweet little girl didn't need rescuing after all.

She wasn't all that sweet either.

Dudley had only just gotten his breath back when he realized that he couldn't see Daphne anywhere.

"Oh, dear," thought Dudley, feeling a little bit scared.

Then he made another big decision. "Dudley, the brave and heroic dog, bravely decides to go for a walk by himself."

Then Dudley happened to notice a hoop to jump through, like at the circus.

"Dudley, the brave circus dog, jumps through the fiery hoop . . . and the crowd gasps!"

But that didn't go well either.

Dudley swung sadly back and forth in

the gentle breeze.

Then he spotted the hot-dog stand.

"Dudley, the brave guard dog, bravely guards the hot dogs!"

Dudley's belly decided that it was lunchtime.

Oh, dear.

Chapter Five

After a large lunch, Dudley lay in
the daisies and thought some very
big thoughts.

"It's dawned on me," said Dudley to
himself, "that being brave and heroic
isn't very easy at all."

Then he spotted some birds.

"Dudley, the sheepdog, bravely rounds
up the flock of sheep . . . um, birds!"
But the birds really didn't want to be
rounded up.

Dudley didn't stop running until he was far, far away.

He was feeling very sad.

When he looked at his reflection in a puddle, all he saw was a scaredy dog looking back.

"Dudley, the brave and heroic dog, isn't brave and heroic after all," he said with a sigh.

"He's just plain old scaredy-dog Dudley, just like Daphne said."

"But it would be nice . . ." he thought, as a tear plopped down, " . . . it would be very nice if Daphne was here to give me a hug and a kiss."

Chapter Six

And guess what?

"Dudley!" squeaked Daphne. "I've

been looking for you everywhere.

I thought you were lost forever!"

She gave him a hug and a kiss. "I love you, you silly old dog," she said with a smile. And, of course, Dudley loved Daphne right back!

"Come on. Let's go home," said Daphne.

They had just gotten to the park gates
when it started to rain.

Oh, dear. Daphne didn't have her
raincoat.
"But it's just a few drops," she said.
Then there were a few more . . . and a
few more . . . and then it was pouring!

"Quick, Dudley, run!" cried Daphne.
And they ran down the street, not
looking where they
were going.
Suddenly, there
was Attila!
They had taken
the wrong way
back home!

Chapter Seven

"ROWWRR!" growled Attila, and he pulled and pulled on the tattered old piece of rope.

Pull! . . . Pull! . . . Pull! . . . Pull! . . . Snap!

The rope broke,
and Attila came
charging at
them, with his
mean eyes and
his sharp,
pointy teeth.

Daphne was
really scared!
She didn't
know what
to do.

Dudley did.

He stood in front of Daphne, took a

deep breath, and . . .

ROOOOOWWWWRRRRR!

It was the loudest growl that Daphne had ever heard.

It was the loudest growl that Attila had ever heard.

It might even have been the loudest growl in the whole world!

Everything was quiet.

Daphne looked at Dudley.

Dudley didn't look like Dudley.

His fur was sticking up, and he
was even fiercer and more snarly
than Attila.

Attila took one look at Dudley,
turned around . . . and ran off!

Chapter Eight

"Dudley, you saved me!" shrieked Daphne, and she gave Dudley a hug and a kiss.

"You're not a scaredy dog anymore," she said with a smile. "You're brave, and you're my hero too!" She gave him another hug and a kiss, just in case she hadn't hugged and kissed him enough the first time.

"I love you, Dudley," she said.

And, of course, Dudley loved Daphne
right back!

But, suddenly, . . . Dudley was gone!

"Dudley? Dudley, where are you?"

Unfortunately, just at that moment,

Dudley thought he had spotted a big,

blue, hairy boggle . . .

. . . and he was still scared of those!

About the author and illustrator

Andy Ellis

This is a portrait of the artist (and writer) as a rabbit.
When he's not a rabbit, Andy likes to write and illustrate
children's books. He also creates animation series and
paints pictures of landscapes. It was while
he was a rabbit that he met Dudley and Daphne and
they told him this story. "It took a long time," says
Andy, "because rabbits find it quite hard
to hold a pencil."

P. S. Don't be scared of spiders. Spiders are our friends!

Strategies for Independent Readers

Predict

Think about the cover, illustrations, and the title
of the book. What do you think this book will be about?
While you are reading think about what may
happen next and why.

Monitor

As you read ask yourself if what you're reading makes sense.
If it doesn't, reread, look at the illustrations, or read ahead.

Question

Ask yourself questions about important ideas
in the story such as what the characters might
do or what you might learn.

Phonics

If there is a word that you do not know, look carefully
at the letters, sounds, and word parts that you do know.
Blend the sounds to read the word. Ask yourself if this is
a word you know. Does it make sense in the sentence?

Summarize

Think about the characters, the setting where the
story takes place, and the problem the characters faced
in the story. Tell the important ideas in the beginning,
middle, and end of the story.

Evaluate

Ask yourself questions like: Did you like the story?
Why or why not? How did the author make the story
come alive? How did the author make the story fun to
read? How well did you understand the story? Maybe
you can understand it better if you read it again!